Virgie Goes to School
with Us Boys

by Elizabeth Fitzgerald Howard ∼ illustrated by E. B. Lewis

Aladdin Paperbacks
New York London Toronto Sydney

Virgie was always begging to go to school with us boys.
All summer long she kept asking and asking.

"School's too far," Nelson said.
"School's too long," Will said.
"School's too hard," George said.
"And you too little," Val said.
"I'm big enough. Tell them, C.C.," Virgie said to me.

"Virgie," Val kept right on, "you scarcely big as a field mouse.
And school's seven miles from here! That's one long, long walk. . . ."
"And besides," Nelson added, "we have to live at school all week!
You couldn't do that. You'd be crying for Mama and all!"
"Nelson, you know I won't be crying for Mama." Virgie stamped
her foot.
"Well anyway," Nelson continued, "there's hardly any girls that go.
Girls don't need school."
"That's not so, Nelson," I said. "Girls need to read and write
and do 'rithmetic too. Just like us boys."

Now didn't I tell you about our school?
For two years us boys—that's George and Will and Nelson and Val and me, C.C.—
been schooling at a place started by some folks who love the Lord.
Quakers, they call themselves.

They opened a school for black people after Mr. Lincoln
declared us free like we ought to be.
And I was beginning to wonder,
What about Virgie?
She was free too.
Couldn't she go to school with us boys?

Summertime going by,
one week gone,
and then another
with Virgie asking and asking . . .

Virgie picking pole beans or weighing grain for Papa.
Virgie sewing quilt squares or stirring soap for Mama.
Virgie always asking,
"Papa, Mama, can I go too?
Can I go to school?"

"Virgie, you'd be all tuckered out just getting there," Will said.
"Raw Head and Bloody Bones might grab you in those
woods on the way!" Nelson said. "Eat up a little old girl."
But Virgie never blinked an eye. She kept right on asking.
Till one day in the fields, Papa said,
"Boys, Virgie, me and your ma been thinking.
All free people need learning—
Old folks, young folks . . . small girls, too.
Virgie, next school time you can go.
You can go to school with the boys."

Summer over.
Harvest in.
School time here!
Sunday night everything ready.
Clean pair of underdrawers for each of us.
Extra shirt too.
And food for the whole week long.
Everything ready, but Nelson was frowning.
"Virgie's too little," he said.

Monday morning early
Mama cooked us big bowls of cornmeal. She cooked eggs, too.
Papa led our prayers. Safe journey. Clear minds.
And thanks to the good Lord for our own school.
"Take care of Virgie," Papa said after prayer time.
"And take care of each other."

Giving orders, George took the lead.
"Not too fast. Stay in a line."
We passed by our barn and Papa's mill,
then cut through Mr. McKinney's field.
"Virgie, keep up now," Val said.
Past old Mr. Smith's farm,
'round Dickson's pond.
"Whoa, Virgie, careful there," Will said. "That's poison ivy."

Up one hill
and down another,
up and down,
down to the creek.

We took off our shoes, rolled up our pants legs,
and stepped real careful on the upping stones.
The cold water woke our hot tired feet.
Virgie held her skirt with one hand, her shoes and bucket with the other.
Then all of a sudden she was sliding and slipping.
"Watch out, Virgie!" I yelled, trying to grab her, but . . .

Splash! In the creek she went.
"Now she'll cry," Nelson grumbled. But she didn't.
Virgie was laughing! "It's a warm day," she said. "My skirt will dry."
Virgie's all right, I thought.

"Let's go!" said George.
"Hurry up!" said Will. "It's looking like rain!"

Just when we were coming to the woods.
It's thick and leafy in there . . . dark even when the sun's bright.
And it's too quiet, but that's not the worst part.
Raw Head and Bloody Bones!
Didn't I tell you about Raw Head and Bloody Bones?
Get you if you're not good, folks said.
Might get you anyway.
"Don't be scared, Virgie," I told her.
"I'm not scared," she said, but she held my hand tight.
Nobody talked. We just walked. Silent 'cept for twigs crackling.

Trees leaned over us. Shadows got darker.
A branch snatched ahold of my shirt, and my heart quit beating.
Then Virgie whispered, "Let's sing!"

"Just like a girl!" Nelson said.
But pretty soon he was singing too. "Go Down Moses" and "Oh Freedom"
and "Eyes Have Seen the Glory" and all the songs we could think of.
The walk went faster then. Seemed not so dark.
Soon we were out of the woods
and away from old Raw Head and Bloody Bones!

Across one field
and then another.
"Almost there, Virgie.
Almost to town."

We passed by the Inn and the Courthouse
and the churches and all the shops,
as we followed Main Street to the top of the hill.
"Do you see it, Virgie? Do you see it?"
We were almost shouting.

Big.
Red brick.
Long high windows and
a wide-open door.
Our very own school.
Mr. Warner the headmaster came out to greet us.

"Welcome, boys. George, William, Valentine, Nelson, Cornelius. (That's me, C.C.)
Glad to see you back. And who is this fine young lady here? Your sister?"
"Yes sir, this is Virgie," George said. "Virgie, speak up to Mr. Warner."
"Good morning, sir," Virgie said.
"Virgie's pretty smart for a girl, Mr. Warner," Nelson said.
Nelson said that!

"Come look, Virgie," I said, pulling her inside with me.
"See all the desks? See the books?"
Virgie was staring,
staring at everything.

Especially the bookcase.
"So many books!" she said. She touched one softly with her hand.
"Someday I'll read all these books!"
Already Virgie was seeming bigger.

"When we go home on Friday, C.C.," she said,
"we'll tell Mama and Papa all we've learned.
That way might seem like they've been to school too.
Learning to be free,
Just like us."

"Learning to Be Free"

Repression of their natural desire to learn was perhaps the cruelest punishment endured by slaves before the Civil War. During this period, many states had laws which prohibited slaves from learning to read or write. Some learned anyway and, ignoring the severe consequences, they taught others. Because of the prohibitions, as few as ten percent of slaves were literate (Haskins, p. 26).

After the war, during the Reconstruction period, lack of education was the biggest hurdle facing the freed men and women (Haskins, ch. 2). In 1865, the Freedmen's Bureau was created by Congress to assist blacks in the transition to freedom. The group had as a major responsibility the encouraging and overseeing of schools. Blacks themselves set up schools and formed societies to raise money for education. Northern aid societies established hundreds of schools. Religious groups such as the Society of Friends (Quakers) also played a significant role. One school established by the Quakers was the Warner Institute in Jonesborough, Tennessee.

My grandfather, Cornelius C. ("C. C.") Fitzgerald, grew up seven miles from Jonesborough, Tennessee, in a family of six boys and one girl. His brother, Will, shared some facts about their childhood with his daughter, Jessie Fitzgerald Lemon, and she in turn told me: Will and C. C.'s parents had been slaves. Their father was a miller and they lived on a farm in a place called May Day. The older boys and their sister, Virgie, walked through the woods to a Quaker school carrying their food and clothing for the week.

Inspired by Cousin Jessie's enticing tidbits, I visited Jonesborough. A history of the town told about a school founded by Quakers for former slaves, known as the Warner Institute. The building—which has been a Baptist school for girls, a Civil War hospital, a boys' school, a restaurant, and a private home—still stands at the top of Main Street (Fink, p. 132-33). So it is very likely that this school, walking distance from May Day, was that necessary first rung of a ladder for the young Fitzgeralds, a first step in their climb toward real freedom.

The adult lives of my grandfather and his siblings are examples of and tributes to the little-known history of countless African Americans who, equipped with the tools of reading and writing, left their rural beginnings seeking opportunities in the wider world. C. C. attended Berea College in Kentucky before it became segregated. Later he and Will studied law, and Val, medicine, at Howard University. They practiced their professions near Baltimore. Nelson also settled in Baltimore, and sold insurance. George became an undertaker in Johnson City. And John, the youngest son, became a pharmacist in Chicago.

But what about Virgie? Details are scarce. She married a teacher, James Ervin; they had four children. Virgie lived only until her early thirties. Ervin became a principal in Johnson City, and later president of Jarvis Christian College in Hawkins, Texas.

I have portrayed Virgie as an independent, spirited young girl who despite the typical skepticism of her older brothers and cautious hesitancy of her parents is determined to claim her right to "go to school with the boys." I think of her as a symbol of that basic drive and hope that filled the minds and hearts of new black citizens, determined through education to make their way in a hostile environment. I imagine her as having left a legacy for all children, girls and boys, African American and not, that education will always be the first step in "learning to be free."

Virgie's brothers. (Back row, left to right) George, C. C., and Nelson. (Front row, left to right) Will, Val, and John (not in story).

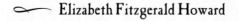 Elizabeth Fitzgerald Howard

Haskins, Jim. *Separate but Not Equal: The Dream and the Struggle.* New York: Scholastic, 1998.
Fink, Paul M. *Jonesborough: The First Century of Tennessee's First Town.* Johnson City, Tenn.: The Overmountain Press, c. 1989.

For Lon with love, first.
And to all Fitzgerald cousins, especially Jessie in Baltimore (who told me
about the long walk), and Gladys and Anne Theodora in Baltimore; to JoAnn
in Jonesborough (with fond thoughts of Gentry); Elizabeth and Lulu in New
York. And to my sister Barbara (Babs). In celebration of Virgie, Will, Val,
George, Nelson, John, and C.C. And Mac, always. —E. F. H.

To my brothers and sisters, who have always
been by my side. —E. B. L.

ALADDIN PAPERBACKS
An imprint of Simon & Schuster Children's Publishing Division
1230 Avenue of the Americas, New York, NY 10020
Text copyright © 2000 by Elizabeth Fitzgerald Howard
Illustrations copyright © 2000 by E. B. Lewis
Also available in a Simon & Schuster Books for Young Readers hardcover edition.
Designed by Lily Malcolm
The text of this book was set in Brighton Medium.
The illustrations were rendered in watercolor.
Manufactured in China
First Aladdin Paperbacks edition January 2005
14 16 18 20 19 17 15
The Library of Congress has cataloged the hardcover edition as follows:
Howard, Elizabeth Fitzgerald.
Virgie goes to school with us boys / by Elizabeth Fitzgerald Howard; illustrated by E. B. Lewis.
p. cm.
Summary: In the post–Civil War South, a young African American girl is determined
to prove that she can go to school just like her older brothers.
ISBN 978-0-689-80076-4 (hc.)
1. Afro-Americans—Juvenile Fiction. 2. United States—History—1849–1877—Fiction.
3. Sex Role—Fiction. 4. Schools—Fiction.] I. Lewis, Earl B., ill. II. Title.
PZ7.H83273Vi 2000
[Fic]—dc21
97-49406
ISBN 978-0-689-87793-3 (Aladdin pbk.)
1117 SCP